Going Out

Lee Davis

Illustrated by Stephen Lewis

Our dog likes to go
out in the snow.

He likes to go fast

on a sledge.

He likes to skate and

he likes to ski.

Our dog likes to go
out in the sun.

He likes to go fast
in a boat.

He likes to swim and

he likes to water-ski.

Best of all, our dog likes
to go out in the rain.

Our dog's name is Mud!

Picture Words

snow

sun

sledge

ski

skate

swim

water-ski

boat

dog

rain